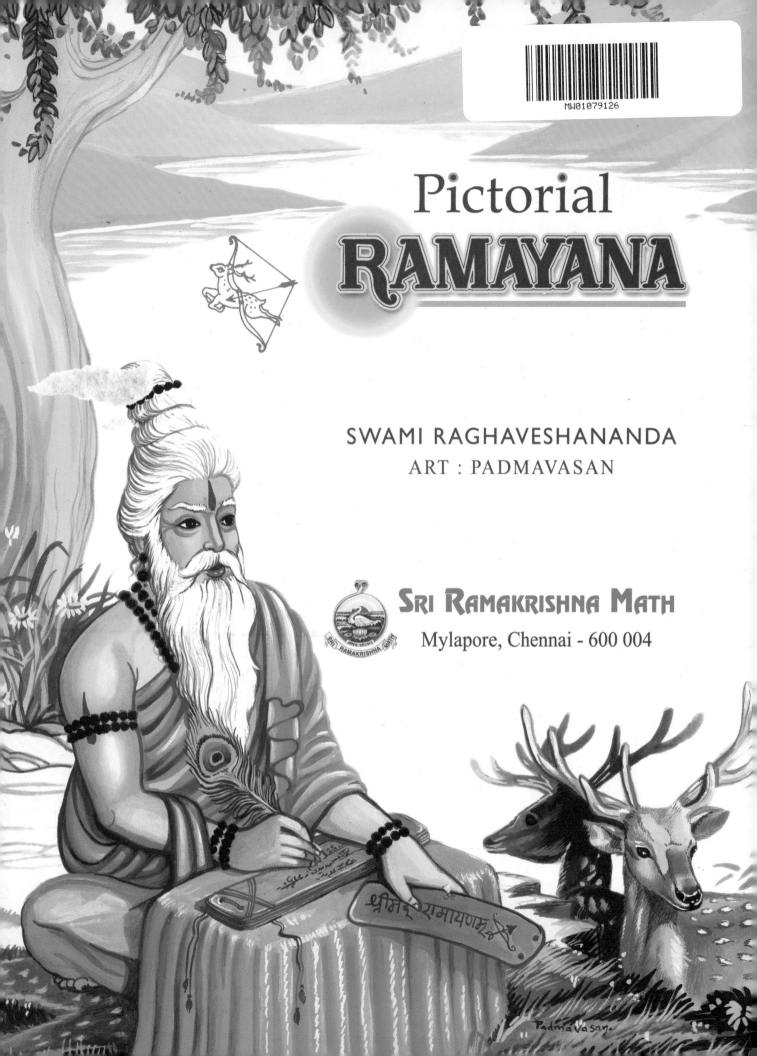

Pictorial
RAMAYANA

SWAMI RAGHAVESHANANDA

ART : PADMAVASAN

SRI RAMAKRISHNA MATH

Mylapore, Chennai - 600 004

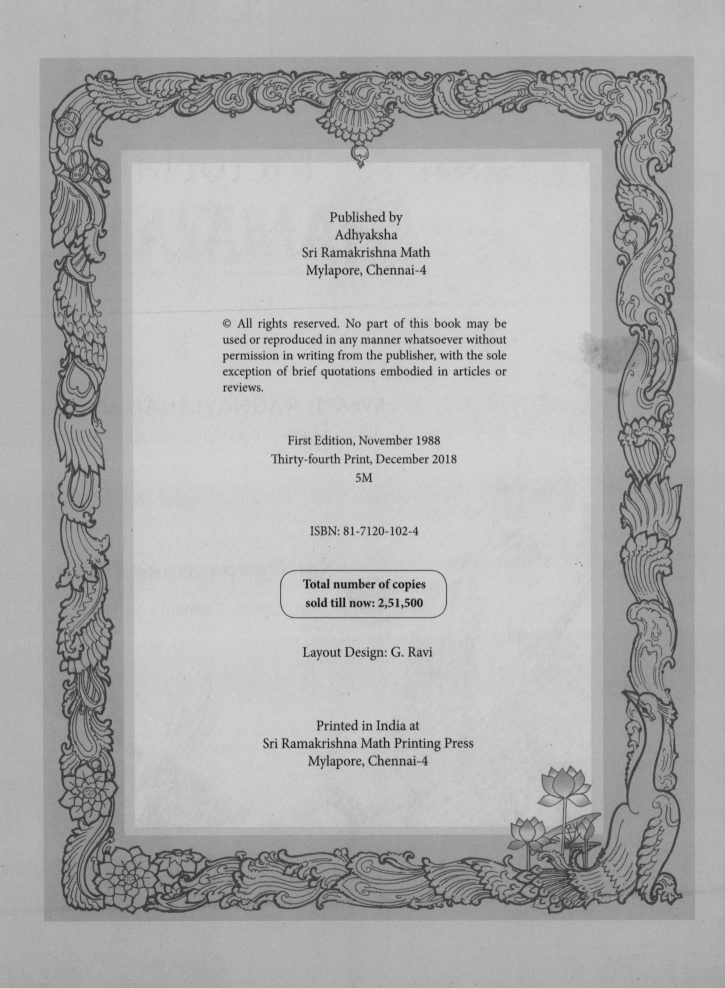

Published by
Adhyaksha
Sri Ramakrishna Math
Mylapore, Chennai-4

First Edition, November 1988
Thirty-fourth Print, December 2018
5M

ISBN: 81-7120-102-4

**Total number of copies
sold till now: 2,51,500**

Layout Design: G. Ravi

Printed in India at
Sri Ramakrishna Math Printing Press
Mylapore, Chennai-4

RAMA IS BORN

DASARATHA was the king of Kosala. His capital was Ayodhya. He hailed from the famous Ikshvaku dynasty. He was loved by all because he cared for the happiness and prosperity of his subjects. Even though Dasaratha had everything to make him happy, he was very sad because he had no children.

Ravana was a great Rakshasa (demon) king. He was so powerful that he persecuted even the gods in heaven. All the gods, led by Brahma approached Lord Vishnu. Brahma said,

'O Lord! Please be kind enough to kill Ravana and protect us.' Vishnu smiled and said, 'Don't worry, I will take birth as Dasaratha's son and kill Ravana.'

In order to have children, Dasaratha performed a great sacrifice with the help of the sage Rishyasringa. He poured ghee on the sacrifical fire while sages led by Rishyasringa chanted the Vedic hymns. When the ritual was about to be over, a celestial being rose from the sacrifical fire. He handed over a bowl to Dasaratha saying, 'O Dasaratha, the gods are pleased with you and have sent you this heavenly payasa (sweet gruel). Give this to your wives and your wish will be fulfilled.

'The king received the gift joyfully and distributed the payasa to his three wives. In due course, four god-like sons were born to him. Rama was the eldest of them. He was born to Kausalya, the first wife of Dasaratha. He was the incarnation of Lord Vishnu. The other three were: Bharata born to Kaikeyi, his second wife, and the twins Lakshmana and Satrughna born to Sumitra his third wife.

The day of Rama's birth is celebrated now as Ramanavami.

SAGE VISWAMITRA VISITS AYODHYA

THE four sons of Dasaratha grew up tall, handsome and brave. Sage Vasishtha was their guru. They learnt the Vedas from him. They also became adept in hunting, riding, fencing, and archery.

The princes were now fifteen years old. Dasaratha loved all of them dearly. But, Rama

was dearest to his heart. Rama and Lakshmana were inseparable companions. Similarly, Bharata and Satrughna always remained together.

One day, the great sage Viswamitra came to Ayodhya. Dasaratha was overjoyed to have the great rishi as his guest. He immediately got down from his throne and received him with great respect. Dasaratha said, 'I am indeed blessed by your visit. Is there anything within my power that I can do for you?' Viswamitra replied, 'O king, I am pleased by your words. Powerful demons are disturbing my sacrifice. I want you to send Rama with me to protect my sacrifice.'

Dasaratha was taken aback by the words of Viswamitra. How could he think of sending young Rama to face the demons? He said, 'O sage, please spare Rama. I shall come with you with my large army and kill myself the demons. Rama is too young for this task'.

But, Viswamitra knew better. He insisted on his request being granted. Sage Vasistha assured Dasaratha that Rama would be safe in the hands of Viswamitra. Ultimately, Dasaratha agreed to send Rama with Viswamitra.

IN THE FOREST

WITH the blessings of Dasaratha, Rama and Lakshmana followed Viswamitra to the forest. 'This is the Dandaka forest,' Viswamitra told the princes, 'Here lives a Rakshasi (female demon) called Tataka with her son Maricha. She has the strength of a thousand elephants. She knows charms and spells too. So, none dares to enter the forest fearing her. Only you can kill her.' At first, Rama hesitated to kill a woman. But, he was reminded of his father's instruction to obey Viswamitra implicitly. So, he strung his bow and twanged the string. The sound echoed in the forest and the wild animals ran helter-skelter in fear. Tataka also heard the sound. She was furious. Who was it that dared to disturb her? Mad with rage and roaring like thunder she rushed towards Rama. A fierce war between Rama and Tataka followed. She began to throw stones and rocks at Rama. But, Rama pierced her heart with a deadly arrow. Tataka crashed to the

earth. Viswamitra rejoiced at Rama's great skill, and decided to give Rama and Lakshmana the divine weapons he had acquired through his austerities. He taught them several mantras, meditating on which divine weapons could be summoned for use.

Then the three proceeded Siddhasrama, the place of Viswamitra. The rishis there entertained Rama and Lakshmana. Viswamitra took a vow of silence and began an elaborate sacrifice. The hermits requested Rama to guard the sacrifice. They were afraid that huge demons Maricha and Subahu would disturb the sacrifice. Rama and Lakshmana fully armed guarded the place day and night. Six days and nights passed without any incident. On the seventh day, when the sacrifice was nearing completion, a terrible noise was heard. Rama looked up and saw Maricha and Subahu along with other demons covering the sky. They were about to pour blood and filth into the sacrificial fire to defile it. But, Rama and Lakshmana were alert. Rama silently prayed and discharged the newly-acquired divine weapons. With one arrow he hurled Maricha miles away into the sea. and with the second one, he killed Subahu. With the help of Lakshmana he killed the other demons too. Viswamitra completed the sacrifice and the sages rejoiced and blessed the princes.

RAMA WEDS SITA

NEXT morning, Viswamitra informed Rama that all the sages were going to Mithila, the capital of the famous King Janaka, to witness a great sacrifice. Rama and Lakshmana too accompanied the sages led by Viswamitra.

Janaka was a saintly king. Once while he was ploughing the land, a lovely baby girl arose from the furrow. He took her home and brought her up as his own daughter and named her Sita.

Janaka had with him a bow given by Lord Siva. The bow was so heavy that it needed many people to move it. Janaka wanted Sita to marry the bravest and the best prince in the country. So, he had vowed that he would give Sita in marriage only to the one who could string that great bow of Lord Siva. Many had tried earlier. But, none could move it, let alone string it.

Janaka was overjoyed to hear about the coming of Viswamitra. He welcomed the party

with great respect. Viswamitra introduced Rama and Lakshmana to Janaka and said, 'Show the great bow to Rama.' Janaka agreed doubtfully. 'The princes are so young and tender. How can they even lift it?' he thought. But he said, 'If Rama can string the bow, I shall gladly get my daughter married to him.' He ordered the bow to be brought in. The bow was kept in a big box mounted on an eight-wheeled chariot. It was pulled by many soldiers into the great hall.

Rama then stood up in all humility. With the permission of Janaka and Viswamitra he opened the box and looked at the bow. Everyone was watching, but none except Viswamitra believed that Rama would be able to string the bow. Rama then lifted the bow with ease. Placing one end against his toe, he put forth his might and bent the bow to string it, when lo! the famous bow snapped into two.

Dasaratha was informed. He gladly gave his consent to the marriage and came to Mithila with his retinue. Janaka arranged for a grand wedding. Rama married Sita. At the same time, Lakshmana married Sita's sister Urmila Bharata and Satrughana married Sita's cousins Mandavi and Srutakirti. Viswamitra blessed them all and left for the Himalayas austerities. Dasaratha returned to Ayodhya with his sons and daughters-in-law.

At Ayodhya

FOR twelve years, Rama lived happily with Sita in Ayodhya. The people of Ayodhya loved Rama as he shared their joys and sorrows. When King Dasaratha

saw that Rama had won the hearts of his people, he decided to install him as the crown prince. Dasaratha was getting old and he wanted Rama to take over the reins of the government. Calling his ministers, he told them of his desire and sought their advice. They unanimously welcomed the suggestion. Dasaratha then ordered for immediate coronation of Rama. At that time Bharata and Satrughna had gone to Kekaya to see their maternal grandfather.

But, there was one woman who grieved to hear about Rama's coronation. It was Manthara. She was Kaikeyi's maid servant. She resolved to stop the coronation somehow or other. She rushed to Kaikeyi. She was the first to give the news of the coronation to Kaikeyi. At first, Kaikeyi was overjoyed to hear that Rama was to be crowned as the king. She loved Rama very much. But, Manthara poisoned her mind. She said, 'What a fool you are! Are you not able to see the sorrow in store for you! The king had always loved you more than the other queens. But, the moment Rama is crowned, Kausalya will be more powerful and take revenge on you. In fact, you are going to become the slave of Kausalya.'

Fear gripped the heart of Kaikeyi. What should she do now? Again, Manthara was there to suggest a plan. She said, 'Remember, long ago when Dasaratha was sorely wounded in a battle with demons, you swiftly drove his chariot to safety and thus saved his life. At that time, he had offered you two boons. You said you would ask for these boons later. Now, the time has come to demand those boons. Choose the coronation of Bharata as the first boon and the banishment of Rama to the forest for fourteen years as the second boon.' Thus, Manthara poisoned the mind of Kaikeyi. The queen, though noble in heart so long, was trapped by Manthara.

THE HELPLESS DASARATHA

DASARATHA came to Kaikeyi's apartments to convey personally the glad news of Rama's installation. Kaikeyi was not in her usual place. When he found her, he was shocked to see her lying on the bare ground with loose hair and all ornaments cast away. He guessed there was something wrong. He gently took her head on his lap and, caressing her, asked her who had done her wrong.

But, Kaikeyi did not care for the king's love and concern toward her. Releasing herself free from his arms she stood up and said, 'You had promised me two boons. Please grant them now. Let Bharata be crowned as king and Rama be banished from the kingdom for fourteen years.'

Dasaratha could hardly believe his ears. Unable to bear what he had heard, he fell down unconscious. Regaining his senses after a while, he looked at Kaikeyi. He was trembling like a deer facing a tiger. He cried out in helpless anger, 'What has come over you? What harm has Rama done to you? You know Rama loves you more than his own mother. You also know that I cannot live without Rama. I clasp your feet. Change your mind and ask for some other boons.' But, Kaikeyi refused to yield. The old king fainted and whole night passed thus. The next morning Sumantra the minister, came to inform Dasaratha that all the preparations for Rama's coronation were ready. Dasaratha was not in a position to speak. But Kaikeyi ordered Sumantra to call Rama immediately. Rama came and saw that the atmosphere was tense. Dasaratha could only say with a voice choked with emotion, 'Rama, Rama, dearest Rama.' Rama was alarmed. He looked at Kaikeyi and said, 'Mother, is father angry with me? Have I offended him in any way? I have never seen him like this before!'

Kaikeyi said, 'He has something unpleasant for you. But, he is afraid to say it. Long ago he had offered me two boons. Now I demanded them.' Kaikeyi told him about the boons. 'Is that all, mother?' asked Rama with a smile. 'Send for Bharata. It does not matter to me in the least whether I am crowned or Bharata, my beloved brother, is crowned. Please take it that your boons are granted. I shall start for the forest today itself.'

RAMA LEAVES FOR THE FOREST

THE news that Rama would leave for the forest spread like wildfire. Everyone was shocked. Lakshmana said angrily, 'Father has been most unjust to you. I will not tolerate this.' Saying so he took up his big bow and started angrily towards Dasaratha's palace. Rama placed his hand on his brother's shoulder. With a gentle smile he said, 'For this small kingdom's sake you want to go against father's word given to Kaikeyi?'

Tears Flowed from Lakshmana's eyes. He said, 'If you must go to the forest, then take me also with you.' Rama agreed.

Rama went to Sita to break the news. He said, 'Look after mother Kausalya in my absence.' She replied, 'Please don't leave me behind. I shall die without you.' with eyes filled with tears. At last, Rama permitted her to follow him. The city was plunged in gloom. Women and children and even men and elders wept at the thought of parting from Rama.

Rama, Sita and Lakshmana sat in the chariot dressed like hermits. The people of Ayodhya ran behind the chariot crying loudly. Sumantra drove the chariot as fast as he could. They reached the bank of the river called Tamasa. The people of Ayodhya followed them. Rama decided to spend the night there. Early next morning, he woke up and told Sumantra, 'The citizens who have followed us are fast asleep. It is not good that they follow me. Let us start before they wake up.'

Rama, Lakshmana and Sita driven by Sumantra, continued their journey. After travelling the whole day, they reached the bank of the Ganga and decided to spend the night there. They sat under a tree. There lived nearby a hunter chieftain called Guha. He felt sad about the happenings. He told Rama, 'Stay with me here, please. My kingdom, my riches and my life are all at your service.'

Rama was touched by his friendship. He said, 'Dear brother, I know how deep is the love you have for me. But, I have promised Kaikeyi that I would live a hermit's life in the forest. We shall live on roots and fruits.'

They slept under a tree that night. Lakshmana and Guha kept watch throughout.

The next morning, the three took leave of Guha and got into the boat. Sumantra came to Rama with a heavy heart. Rama Said, 'Go back to Ayodhya and console my father.'

As Rama's boat sailed away, Sumantra and Guha looked on with tears in their eyes.

Bharata's Return to Ayodhya

AFTER three days, Sumantra returned with a heavy heart to Ayodhya and went straight to Dasaratha. There he found the king more dead than alive. He bent his head in silence and Dasaratha understood.

'Oh! Rama! Rama! Rama!' he cried in pain. That very night Dasaratha died of a broken heart. His body was preserved in oil. Vasishtha sent messengers to Kekaya to bring Bharata and Satrughna back. They were instructed not to give any indication of what had happened.

Bharata immediately returned with Satrughna. As he entered the city, he saw bad omens. He found the city strangely silent. When he came to Dasaratha's

palace, he found it empty. He then hurried to Kaikeyi. When he saw her face sad and pale, he knew something was wrong.

'Where is father?' he cried. She said, 'My son, he has gone to the abode of the gods.' 'Dead!' Bharata was stunned by the news. 'Father is dead! How? Why? When? Why did they not send for me earlier?' he cried aloud in a fit of grief. He asked, 'Where is Rama? He was at least lucky to be with father and hear his last words. Did my father leave any message for me?' 'His last words were, "Rama" ', replied Kaikeyi. Bharata was surprised.

'Was he not present when the king died?' he asked.

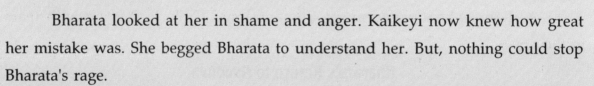

She replied, 'My son, Rama has been banished to the forest for fourteen years.' And she narrated the whole story to him.

Bharata could not believe his ears. He understood everything and realized the disaster caused by his mother.

Bharata looked at her in shame and anger. Kaikeyi now knew how great her mistake was. She begged Bharata to understand her. But, nothing could stop Bharata's rage.

He said angrily, 'You are my enemy, not my mother, Oh! You heartless woman, you have killed my father; you have banished my brother. Did you not know how much I love Rama? I do not wish to have anything to do with you. I am no longer your son.' So saying, he rushed to Kausalya's apartment.

Kausalya and Sumitra welcomed him. Kausalya full of sorrow, spoke in a low voice, 'Bharata, the kingdom is waiting for you. You need not fear any opposition from us. All that we request you to do is to take me, and Sumitra to the forest to live with Rama.'

Tears trickled down Bharata's face as he heard her. He fell at the feet of Kausalya and clasping them with both his hands cried sobbing, 'Mother You know, my love for Rama. Is is right for you to say these words? I can never accept the crown that belongs to Rama.' He promised her that he would bring Rama back to Ayodhya.

BHARATA MEETS RAMA

DAY and night, Bharata thought of Rama and how to bring him back. He knew no peace. He asked Vasishta for advice. Vasishta told him that the funeral rites of Dasaratha could not be delayed. Arrangements were made with the permission of Bharata for the cremation of the body. Holy men chanted the funeral hymns and Bharata lighted the pyre with appropriate rituals.

When the rites were completed, Bharata made up his mind to go in search of Rama. He left Ayodhya with a large army and entered the forest. Kaikeyi and other queens also followed him. After many days they reached Chitrakuta.

Halting the army at a distance, Bharata went to meet Rama. He fell at Rama's feet, sobbing. Rama embraced Bharata and kissed him on the head, and said, 'Why did you leave our father and come to the forest? Why have you grown so thin?' Bharata could not answer. Again, Rama asked him many questions. But, Bharata remained silent and started weeping.

After an interval, gaining strength Bharata replied 'Brother, our father has gone to heaven soon after you left. Come back with me, wear the crown and accept the kingdom.'

When Rama heard that his father was dead, he swooned. Sita sprinkled water on his face and helped him recover. After sometime he rose, and they all went to the river Mandakini to offer prayers for their departed father.

Next day, Bharata repeatedly begged Rama to return to Ayodhya. But, Rama firmly replied, 'I will not disobey my father at any cost. You go back and rule the kingdom. And I, for my part, shall carry out my pledge and come back after fourteen years.' But Bharta could not be turned away so easily. At last, Vasishtha found a solution. He said,' O Bharata, rule the kingdom with Rama's authority and as his deputy.' Bharata knew he had to be content with this. But, he could not think of sitting on the throne that rightfully belong to Rama. 'Dear Rama,' he said, 'I see that I must obey you, but let me take back something that belongs to you.' Rama gracefully agreed. Bharata then took his brother's sandals and carried them back to Ayodhya on his head with great reverence. He placed the sandals on the throne and ruled the kingdom in Rama's name, staying in a little hut and counting the days for Rama's return.

THE COMING OF SURPANAKHA

WHEN Bharata left, Chitrakuta lost all its former attraction for Rama. The trio left Chitrakuta and spent the next few years wandering through the great forest, visiting the holy men on the way. Sage Agastya advised Rama to settle at Panchavati

on the banks of the Godavari. On reaching Panchavati, Lakshmana built an elegant hut. They lived happily there.

One day, Ravana's sister Surpanakha saw Rama and, struck by his beauty, fell in love with him. She approached him and said, 'I am Surpanakha, the sister of Ravana, the king of the Rakshasas. Two of my brothers Khara and Dushana are the lords of Janasthana not far from here. I long to marry you. Do not warry about this girl. I shall eat her up immediately.'

Rama was too amused to be angry with her. Smilingly he said, 'As you see I am already married. But, my brother Lakshmana has not got his wife with him. He is young and handsome. Approach him, O fair lady.' Surpanakha took Rama's word seriously and approached Lakshmana. Lakshmana understood the joke. He said, 'Rama is my master. I am his slave. It is not proper that you should become a slave of a slave.' Surpanakha again went to Rama, but this time with flaming eyes, she said, 'You are humiliating me in the presence of this woman. I will now devour her before your very eyes.' So saying, she pounced upon Sita like a wild animal. But, Lakshmana swiftly intervened and cut off her nose. Surpanakha, crying with pain, ran away into the forest to seek the help of her brother Khara.

In a short time, she returned with fourteen Rakshasas to attack Rama. But, they were killed by Rama in no time. Khara, red with anger, ordered fourteen thousand of his army to march against Rama with all their chariots, horses and elephants. He asked his brother Dushana and other generals to accompany him. Rama decided to face the demons single-handed. He asked Lakshmana to protect Sita. He put on his armour, took the bow and arrows and destroyed the entire army. A shining arrow pierced the heart of Dushana. Mad with anger at seeing the destruction of Dushana, Khara rushed against Rama. He turned his chariot and drove against Rama. Even before Rama was aware, he discharged a sharp arrow and cut Rama's bow into two. Rama was surprised. Before he could take up another bow, seven more arrows came from Khara and broke his armour to pieces. His body was now exposed. Khara took advantage of this and sent arrow after arrow which hurt Rama in different parts of the body. But fearless Rama took the great bow given by Agastya and discharged thirteen arrows in quick succession, which killed the demon. The battle had lasted an hour and a quarter. Sita and Lakshmana were thrilled to see Rama's valour. Sita ran to him and embraced him with tears of joy in her eyes.

THE GOLDEN DEER

SURPANAKHA was terror-stricken and flew to Lanka to seek the protection of Ravana. Ravana was shocked to see his sister disfigured. He asked her for the cause. Surpanakha narrated how Khara and Dushana and their whole army had been destroyed. 'Brother!' she said, 'I was all anxious to get the beautiful Sita for you. But your brothers were killed in that attempt. The best way of punishing Rama is to carry away Sita to Lanka. Rama would then die of grief, as he would never know the whereabouts of Sita.'

Quick as lightning Ravana thought of a plan that would avenge the insult his sister has suffered and at the same time get the lovely Sita for himself. He set out in his plane Pushpaka. First, he went to Maricha and sought his help to abduct Sita. When Maricha heard Rama's name he trembled; for how could he forget the death of his mother Tataka at Rama's hands? He stared at Ravana in horror. 'You have been misled about Rama' he said. 'Years ago, I used to torment Viswamitra. At that time Rama came there. And do you know what he did? With one arrow he killed Subahu and with another he hurled me far into the sea. He was a mere boy then. Now he is grown up and strong. Do not plan your own ruin. And do not, I pray, have any thoughts of Sita. She is chastity personified. Her anger will reduce you to ashes.' But, Ravana refused to heed Maricha's advice. 'I have come here to seek your help and not advice,' he said, 'Now take your choice. Help me in my plan or prepare for death.' Maricha knew that his end was near. He thought for the while and then said, 'I would rather be killed by Rama than by you.' So saying he got ready for a wicked trick.

Sita was gathering flowers near her cottage when a golden deer flashed past. Sita was spellbound. 'Do come and look,' she cried, eager that Rama and Lakshmana should see that beautiful deer. They came out looking in all directions. Sita, pointing to the animal, cried with delight, 'Look! I have never seen such a beautiful deer in my life. Can you get it for me? I will make it my pet.' 'It is a wonderful creature,' said Rama, 'Lakshmana we must catch it, as Sita is so delighted with it and wants it.'

Lakshmana grew suspicious. He said, 'This is not an animal. It seems that demons are playing tricks on us.' But Rama said, 'If this deer is a real animal, I shall get it for Sita. But if it is a demon, I shall kill him. Have no fear, but look after Sita. Take care, don't leave her, whatever happens.' With these words, Rama started out in pursuit of the golden deer.

The golden deer was none other than Maricha. It ran swiftly into the deep forest and Rama followed it. At last, when Rama found it not possible to catch it alive he killed it with a sharp arrow.

As Rama's arrow pierced his heart Maricha knew he was going to die. He cried, 'Ah, Sita! Ah, Lakshmana! Help, help!', in a voice resembling Rama's, and fell down dead. Sita was thunderstruck. It was her husband's voice. She said to Lakshmana, 'Do you not hear your brother's voice? Probably he is surrounded by demons and needs your help. Go at once to his help.' But, Lakshmana was calm and unmoved. 'Don't be alarmed, O princess,' he replied, 'It is all the trick of demons. Rama would never cry like that.'

But, Sita would not listen. She forced Lakshmana to go. At last he left her reluctantly with the warning: 'I shall draw a line. Don't cross this line for any reason. You will be safe as long as you stay within the circle. May the gods protect you!' And with the tip of his arrow, Lakshmana drew a line around the hut and went inside to the forest in search of Rama.

Ravana saw that his trick had worked. Sita was alone. He disguised himself as a hermit, complete with wooden sandals, staff and water pot. Clothed in ochre garment he approached the hermitage, chanting the Vedas. Wondering at the strange voice, Sita came out of the hut. Seeing a holy man, she brought some food and offered it to him, standing within the line drawn by Lakshmana.

'Come nearer to make the offering, daughter,' said Ravana, still standing where he was.

'But I can't,' said Sita, 'I am not permitted to cross this line.'

'In that case I don't need your alms.' With these words Ravana began to walk away.

Sita felt ashamed at failing to entertain a holy man. And, before she quite realized what she was doing, she had stepped outside the magic line and was calling after Ravana.

Immediately Ravana pounced on her and seized her hands. He thundered, 'I am Ravana, the king of Lanka. Come to Lanka and be my queen. There will be five thousand slaves at your service. Leave this beggar Rama and follow me.'

Saying so, he dragged her to his chariot, which flew off into the sky.

RAMA'S SORROW

MEANWHILE, Rama was hurrying back to the hut in great anxiety. He was surprised to see Lakshmana on the way coming in search of him.

'Ah Lakshmana! Why have you left Sita alone?' cried Rama. Lakshmana related the painful circumstances in which he was forced to leave the hermitage. As he listened, Rama knew that a grave danger was in store for Sita. They hurried to the hut and found it empty, even as they feared. They ran from place to place, from tree to tree, from bush to bush. They searched, shouted and called out her name. All in vain. Rama became desperate and began to question every tree, every beast and bird that he came acros. At last, he sat down exhausted on a seat of stones and told Lakshmana that he would never leave that forest. He would die where his Sita had died. Lakshmana tried to console him as best as he could. A little later they again started in search of Sita.

Jatayu, the king of eagles was sitting on a tree when Ravana was carrying away Sita. He was a close friend of Dasaratha. Hearing Sita's cry for help, he flew and fought with Ravana to free Sita. Ravana attacked Jatayu. He shot arrows at the

bird, but disregarding them Jatayu fought on with his beak and talons. The battle was fierce. At last, Ravana cut off the wings of the bird with his sword. Jatayu was helpless. Unable to move, he fell on the ground. Rama and Lakshmana, while searching for Sita, came to the place where Jatayu was lying wounded. Jatayu painfully raised his bleeding head and said, 'O Rama! Sita has been carried away by Ravana. I tried my best to save her. But, the cruel Ravana cut off my wings and flew away with her.' Uttering these words, Jatayu spat blood and died. Rama mourned for the great sacrifice

of Jatayu. He cremated him and duly performed his last rites, as if he were his close relative.

Crossing the sea, Ravana entered Lanka his kingdom. Taking Sita to his palace, he called some maids and ordered them, 'Take charge of this fair lady. Give her food or silks or jewels or precious stones that she wants.' Sita shrank from them like a deer from a pack of hounds. To impress her with his wealth and power, Ravana forcefully took her round his palace and showed her all his glories. He took her to his pleasure garden. But, nothing could win her mind. He said at last, 'Look here, I will give you full year. Think over what I have said. Accept me as your husband.

If at the end of this period you remain stubborn, I shall command my servants to cut you to pieces and serve the meat for my breakfast.' He ordered his servants to keep her in the Ashoka garden and to guard her carefully.

ENCOUNTER WITH KABANDHA

RAMA and Lakshmana continued their search. While wandering in the forest they suddenly heard a terrific noise. They saw a huge monstrous coming out of the bushes He had no head or legs but only a huge trunk covered with hair. He had only one eye in the middle of his breast; and an ugly mouth in his breast, out of which projected two white curved fangs, and between them a lolling tongue dripping blood. He had two long arms, with the help of which, he gathered his prey and thrust it into his mouth

Slowly his two hands moved and encircled Rama and Lakshmana and dragged them towards his mouth. Sensing the danger, they cut off those arms and freed themselves. The monster yelled with pain and panted in a pool of blood. Then he cried, 'Who are you, Sirs?' The question surprised them. Lakshmana told him briefly who they were and asked him whether he could give any information about Sita.

The monster replied, 'My name is Kabandha. Once I had a beautiful form. Due to my ego and pride, I was turned into a monster by a curse. By your grace, I have been freed from the curse. When I die, burn this body to ashes. Then I shall get back my original form, and may be able to foresee things and tell you'.

When the monster died, Rama and Lakshmana burnt it. There arose a celestial being from the ashes. He bowed to Rama and Lakshmana and said, 'O princes! Go West from here and make friendship with Sugriva who is living in Rishyamuka. With his help you will regain Sita. On your way to Rishyamuka you may also visit the hermitage of Sabari.'

RAMA VISITS SABARI

THE next day, the princes travelled towards the hermitage of Sabari on the banks of Lake Pampa. Earlier, sage Matanga with his disciples performed austerities in that hermitage. Sabari had served them devotedly. When they departed from the earth, they instructed her to wait for Rama and serve him. By this she would attain the heavenly abode. Accordingly, this noble woman had waited for two years, living alone. She was always storing choice good nuts, fruits and honey to offer Rama and Lakshmana.

When they went, she immediately recognized that they were her long-expected guests and fell at their feet. She took them inside, washed their feet, and offered them the nuts and fruits. Rama was moved by her devotion. He gently held the old woman's hand and shed tears of joy.

He said, 'O holy Sabari, I am sure, your service to sages and your austerities, have secured you a place in heaven.' Sabari offered him homage and said, 'Yes my Lord, today my austerities have borne fruit, as I have seen you. I waited on this earth only to serve you. Give me permission to depart.' She showed them around the lake and hermitage. Then she gave up her body and passed away in a form of dazzling brightness. The princes bowed and left the hermitage.

SUGRIVA'S FRIENDSHIP

RAMA and Lakshmana walked on until they came to the lovely hill of Rishyamuka.

While they were thus going on their way to the mountain Rishyamuka to meet Sugriva, Sugriva himself saw them from the mountain heights and mistaking them for agents of his dreaded elder brother Vali, fled away to more unapprochable heights. Sugriva was driven out of his kingdom by Vali and had to live in constant fear of him.

Earlier, Vali was king of Kishkindha and Sugriva assisted him. During that time a demon named Mayavi came to the gate of Kishkindha and challenged Vali to a fight. Vali and Sugriva rushed out to fight. When Mayavi saw both of them coming, he fled away in fear. They saw him entering a cave. Vali entered the cave, asking Sugriva to wait at the mouth of the cave. Sugriva waited at the entrance. He heard sounds of a struggle inside and the confused yells of Vali. A stream of blood gushed out from the cave. Sugriva thought that Vali had been overpowered and killed. To prevent the demon from coming out of the cave, he blocked the mouth of the cave with a huge rock. He was in great grief. Since a country cannot be without a king, the ministers persuaded Sugriva to ascend the throne. After a few days suddenly Vali appeared. After killing the giant, he had kicked away the boulder and returned. He thought that Sugriva had treacherously sealed the den and seized the kingdom during his absence. He drove Sugriva out of the kingdom and took away his wife. Ever since, Sugriva had been living in the Rishyamuka hill, which was out of bounds for Vali because of a rishi's curse.

On seeing Rama and Lakshmana, Sugriva sent Hanuman, his trusted friend, to know who the strangers were and why they had come. Hanuman assumed the guise of a young ascetic and came to Rama and Lakshmana. He asked them who they were and why they were wandering in the forest. The brothers told him about themselves and said that they were glad to meet the messenger of Sugriva, the very person they were in search of as friend and ally.

Pleased with their words, Hanuman took off his guise and assuming his original form, carried the brothers on his shoulders to Sugriva. Hanuman narrated Sugriva their story and told him how they had come to seek his alliance.

Sugriva tore off a big branch from a tree. The friends sat on it and began to shave each other's sorrows. Hanuman then kindled a fire to bear witness to the alliance they were making. Rama and Sugriva solemnly went round the fire hand in hand saying, 'Hereafter your sorrow is my sorrow and your joy is my joy.'

Sugriva appealed to Rama, 'I am hiding on this hill fearing Vali. Will you kill Vali and restore my wife to me?' Rama assured him that he would do so.

DEATH OF VALI

SUGRIVA was not sure of Rama's strength. He said to Rama, 'Sir, look at those gigantic Sala trees standing in a row. Vali once discharged series of arrows. Each arrow penetrated the trunk of a tree and came out on the other side. Such is the strength of my brother. I do not know how you can win him.'

Rama rose from his seat saying, 'I think, O Sugriva, I must first create faith in you.' He went near the Sala trees and discharged an arrow, which went straight through the trunks of seven of them standing in a row and fell on the other side and buried itself deep in the ground. Sugriva was filled with amazement.

They all proceeded to Kishkindha, the capital of Vali. In a few hours, they reached the outskirts of the city. The arrangement was that Sugriva should make his appearance at the city gate and challenge Vali to fight, while Rama and others would hide behind. So, Sugriva went up and gave a terrific roar. Vali came out and began to fight with Sugriva. Rama was watching the duel from a distance. He was puzzled to see the

brothers resembled each other very closely. It became impossible for him to identify Sugriva. Hence, he looked on helplessly as Sugriva received thunderous blows of his brother. At last Sugriva ran away, yelling and bleeding. Vali turned back to his capital triumphant. When Rama and Lakshmana came to Sugriva, he spoke in an aggrieved tone, 'If you had told me the truth that you would not kill Vali, I would not have challenged him to fight and got beaten almost to death.' Rama pacified him. He said, 'Both of you looked so alike. It would have been disastrous if I had killed you by mistake. Again challenge Vali. This time wear a garland around your neck so that I can recognize you, and I will surely kill him.' So, they went to Kishkindha again. Sugriva approached the city gate and roared as before, while the rest remained hidden. Now Vali rose in great anger and vowed that he would not let Sugriva escape from his hand. He would mercilessly kill him this time. But, his wife Tara sensed danger and tried to restrain him. She said, 'Your brother who was beaten up yesterday would not come and challenge you again if he were not

sure of some strong help from others. Moreover, I hear from our son Angada that two princes have come to help Sugriva.'

Vali was impatient. He said, 'What are you saying Tara? Don't stand in my way. This is between me and Sugriva, and nobody else should interfere.' Vali came out roaring like a lion. The brothers dashed against each other and fought hand to hand, sometimes rolling on the ground in deadly grip, sometimes flying into the air, tearing at each other. Sometimes they separated only to break the branches of nearby trees. Anticipating Rama's help, Sugriva kept up an equal fight. For long, Rama was watching the valour of Vali. He then sent a sharp arrow which whizzed in the air and went straight to the heart of Vali. Vali fell mortally wounded. Rama with his companions came near Vali. Struggling with death. Vali began to taunt Rama for his cowardly act. He asked, 'Rama, is this your dharma to kill one who is engaged in fighting with another? You are not fit to be a king. If you had wanted help against Ravana, you could have asked me. I would have brought him hand and foot bound and delivered him to you. I am sorry for your action.'

Rama said, 'Vali, you are not fit to talk of dharma. True dharma requires that you should treat your younger brother as your son and his wife as your

daughter. Instead, you have taken Sugriva's wife. It is to maintain dharma that I had to kill you.'

Vali at last saw the error of his ways and commanded his wife and son to the care of Rama. He called Sugriva to his side and said, 'Sugriva. hereafter you will rule the kingdom. Look upon Angada as your son. Take this golden chain from my neck as my last gift to you. It has been given to me by Indra.' Thus, the generous Vali blessed his brother and breathed his last.

SEARCH FOR SITA

SUGRIVA was again crowned king. He was so grateful to Rama that he swore to be his friend and ally for the rest of his life. It was rainy season. So, they had to wait for their next step. When the rains ceased, Lakshmana reminded Sugriva of his vow. Sugriva immediately called his general Neela and said, 'We have to search all over the world for Sita. Order all our powerful armies to assemble immediately.' The monkey armies came and occupied the entire region round the cave of the princes as far the eyes could see. They were in large numbers that they resembled a cloud of locusts. Sugriva surveyed them and said to Rama, 'Our entire army, O Prince, is at your command. You can now give any order you like to test the sincerity of Sugriva.' Rama embraced him in joy and said, 'We should first find out where Sita is. You are the king, so you give orders to your army to search Sita.' Accordingly, Sugriva sent efficient generals with their armies in different directions to search Sita.

Lastly, he called Hanuman and said, 'There is none to equal you, O Hanuman, in strength, valour, swiftness, discrimination, and wisdom. I have great hopes in you. You succeed where others fail. I rely on you to discover the where abouts of Sita.'

When Rama saw what great confidence Sugriva had in Hanuman of whose powers he himself had formed a very high opinion, he gave Hanuman his signet ring and said, 'Take this ring. I am full of hope that you will find Sita. By this token she will, without fear or suspicion, recognize that you have come from me.' Hanuman bent low, touched the feet of Rama and taking the ring from his hand placed it reverently on his head before securing it about his person.

HANUMAN TRAVELS SOUTHWARDS

HANUMAN, Angada, Jambavan and other heroes travelled southwards. Within the allotted time of thirty days all the expeditions returned home, except Hanuman and his party. Those who returned reported that they had searched all possible hiding places in the various lands they visited but could not find any trace of Sita.

Hanuman and a few others went south and searched all forests and mountains but in vain. They were all tired, footsore, and thirsty. In a thick impenetrable forest, they came across what looked like the mouth of a cave from which different kinds

of birds were flying with wings dripping with water. Hoping to find some water, they entered the cave. The passage was totally dark. They must have walked a few miles. There seemed to be no end. It was a trying experience. At last they felt it was getting a little less dark. They emerged into a wide plain full of fruit bearing trees. It was a golden city. The streets were paved with jewels set in gold. They saw an elderly woman who looked like an ascetic. Hanuman asked her respectfully who she was and whether the place belonged to her. She told them that the city originally belonged to a demon called Maya. Indra killed him for his misbehaviour. The city was presented to a celestial damsel called Hema in Indra's court. Hema had entrusted the responsibility to this noble woman.

She fed them sumptuously with delicious refreshments. After the monkeys had eaten she told them, 'No stranger who enters this city can go back from here. You have come on a great mission. So, I will help you. Now close your eyes.' Accordingly, they closed their eyes. When they opened their eyes after some time, they found themselves on the sea shore.

Standing on the shore, they soon realized that the limit of one month imposed on them had already passed. Angada lamented, 'Alas! If we return to the capital without any news about Sita, we shall be put to death. It is better to fast unto death here than to return.' So saying he sat down on the ground. On seeing him the others also sat round him in tears, assuring him that none of them would go back to Kishkindha without their leader and that all would die with him.

MEETING SAMPATI

WHILE they were thus conversing, a huge eagle with broken wings crept out of the mountaSin cave not far away. He rejoiced at the sight of so many creatures. If he killed them at one stroke, he would have ample food for several months. 'We should welcome death at this creature's hands,' said Angada, 'it would be a more merciful death to be killed at one stroke than to starve for a number of weeks. But, our death will not be as glorious as that of Jatayu, who died after fighting with Ravana.'

When the eagle heard the name Jatayu, he addressed the monkeys in their own language, 'Who are you, Sirs? You referred to the death of my beloved brother Jatayu, whom I have not seen for many years. I am Sampati, Jatayu's elder brother.' Jatayu and Sampati were sons of Aruna, the god of dawn. When they were young they competed with each other as to who could fly higher in the sky. They soared higher and higher. As they neared the sun the heat became unbearable and Jatayu was about to be burnt. Quickly Sampati rescued him by spreading his wings over him. But, Sampati's wings were burnt off and he fell on a hill. Since then he had stayed in the same place unable to move. Sampati told that he had seen Ravana carrying Sita. The monkeys were wild with joy on receiving this definite news about Sita. Sampati's troubles also were over. He had received a boon from a rishi that he would get back his wings when he helped Rama. New feathers grew on his body and soon he flew away joyfully.

HANUMAN CROSSES THE OCEAN

THE next problem to them was who among them could leap across the sea to reach Lanka. Angada asked everyone this question and got varied answers. He himself said he could jump and land in Lanka but he would not be able to recross the sea. Hanuman was sitting silently. 'Why are you so quiet, my friend?" asked Jambavan. 'Your strength, courage and wisdom are well known. You can fly like Garuda. There is none equal to you here. Arise, O Hanuman, come forward and put hope and courage into our hearts.'

When Hanuman was thus reminded of his strength, his form began to grow and he was almost touching the sky. He climbed on the Mahendra mountain. There was a roar and a shake when he took off from the mountain at full speed.

The eager faces of the army watched him as he disappeared behind the clouds. Flying was a secret which Hanuman had learnt from his father, Vayu, the God of the winds. As he was travelling, suddenly he felt himself being dragged towards the sea by a great force. He looked down and saw a huge demoness pulling him down. She opened her mouth wide to swallow him. At once, he entered her mouth and ripped his way out through her stomach. The demoness died and sank into the sea. Hanuman again rose and continued his journey.

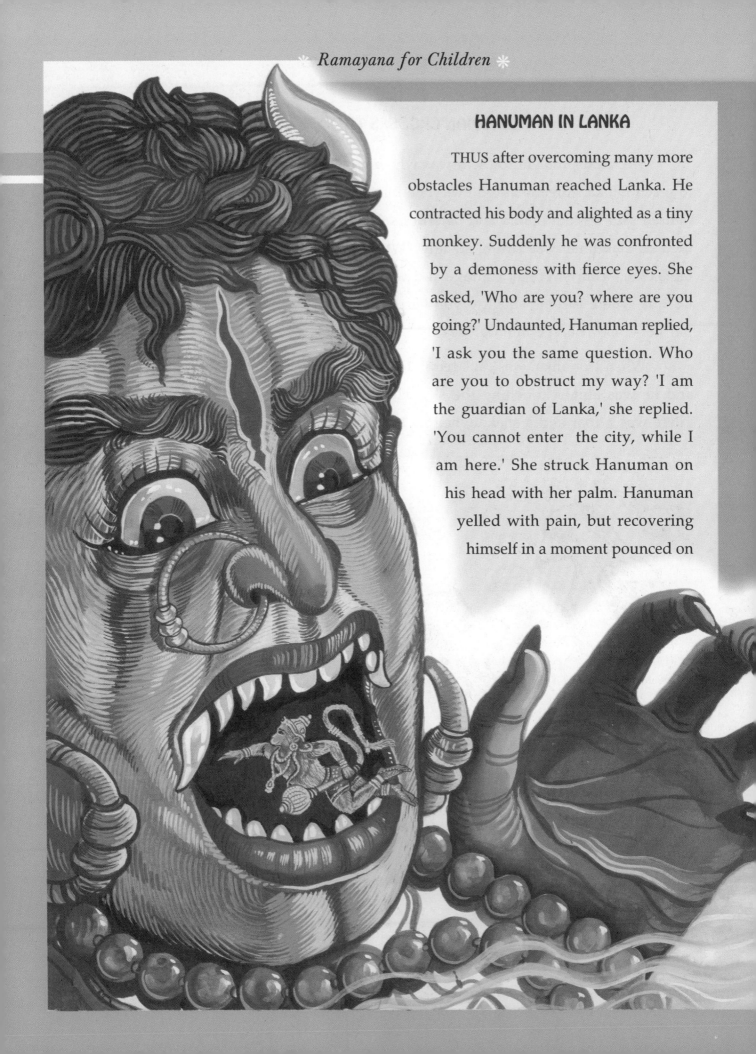

HANUMAN IN LANKA

THUS after overcoming many more obstacles Hanuman reached Lanka. He contracted his body and alighted as a tiny monkey. Suddenly he was confronted by a demoness with fierce eyes. She asked, 'Who are you? where are you going?' Undaunted, Hanuman replied, 'I ask you the same question. Who are you to obstruct my way? 'I am the guardian of Lanka,' she replied. 'You cannot enter the city, while I am here.' She struck Hanuman on his head with her palm. Hanuman yelled with pain, but recovering himself in a moment pounced on

her and dealt her a powerful blow with his fist and she fell down crushed in every limb. She begged for mercy and said, 'You have vanquished me. I now remember a prophecy. When I am defeated, the city of Lanka will be conquered and destroyed.'

Hanuman then cautiously entered the city and went along the main streets. In the evening he managed to enter the palace quietly. He searched chamber after chamber. But Sita could be found. As he wandered about, he came to a wonderful garden called Asokavana. The cool breeze and the delicious fruits of the garden invited him to rest. 'I am very tired' he said to himself, 'I shall rest here for a while and enjoy the fruits here.'

MEETING SITA

SUDDENLY, he saw something shining under a tree. When he looked closer, he found a very beautiful woman sitting there. She was guarded by hideous demonesses. She was thin and emaciated, with no ornaments, dishevelled hair and absolutely careless about her appearance. To Hanuman, she appeared like a raging fire. When she raised her face, to heaven, wet with tears, as if praying for relief, his heart melted in pity, lifting him for a moment above the plane of mortal beings. Gazing at her, Hanuman felt he grew divine. This experience profoundly created an impression upon him. Suddenly, he became an immortal, as it were. And henceforth service to her became the sole aim of his existence. He instinctively felt that this was the Sita he was in search of.

Just then Ravana entered the garden. He approached Sita and said, 'O Fair lady! Why do you shrink from me? Accept me and become the empress of this great land. You have waited all these months in vain hope. You may wait till the end of your life. Rama will not be able to cross the ocean and come to this impregnable

city. Even the gods dare not approach it.' Sita laughed scornfully and said, 'How often have I to tell you that you are doing yourself no good in thus turning your mind to a married woman? Just as you would like your own wives to be pure in mind and faithful to you, should you not wish to see the wives of others pure in mind and faithful to their husbands? If you want to live and rule your kingdom, there is only one way. Return me to my Lord, and beg his pardon.'

Ravana was furious. He thundered, 'What! Me begging to that insignificant human! I see that the more I try to conciliate you, the more you insult me. I have fixed a time for you. There are still two months left. Even at the end of this time if you remain adamant, my cooks will cut you up and serve you for my breakfast.' With these threatening words Ravana hurriedly left the place.

As soon as Ravana left, the demonesses surrounded Sita. One of them said, 'Enjoy the riches of Lanka by accepting Ravana, or else we will kill you without waiting for the two months.' Surrounded by these cruel demonesses, Sita broke down and wept.

Trijata, an old demoness, who had been sleeping till now wake up and restrained them. 'Desist, fools,' she cried, 'trouble her no more. I have had a dream which signifies the triumph of Sita and her husband and the complete destruction of Lanka. This revelation of their friend unnerved them. They left Sita alone and retired to their places.

HANUMAN GIVES THE RING

MEANWHILE, Hanuman, who had been witnessing the happenings from the tree, thought to himself, 'How can I convince her that I am Rama's messenger? If I suddenly appear before her, she will think that it is another one of Ravana's tricks.' He hit upon a plan and began to recite Rama's story in a sweet and gentle voice. Sita was astonished to hear about Rama. She looked up and saw a small monkey perched on a tree. Then Hanuman slowly alighted near her and asked her, 'O Mother, from your sorrow and tears I take you to be a princess. Are you Sita, whom I am searching?' 'Yes,' said Sita, 'I am Sita. You seem to know my husband. May I know who you are?' 'I am the messenger of Rama, I am called Hanuman. I have come here at the command of Rama.'

The words of Hanuman sent a thrill of joy through the heart of Sita. She was anxious to hear more about Rama and Lakshmana. But a doubt crept into her mind. She suspected that the monkeys might be Ravana in disguise. She closed her eyes. Hanuman tried different ways to assure her that he was the messenger of Rama and not Ravana in disguise. He gave a long and eloquent description of the prince and how he met him. He placed in her hand Rama's ring that he had brought. He said, 'Oh, Mother, I shall return and inform Rama about you and bring him immediately. He will release you from this bondage. But why should you suffer any longer? Even now I can carry you across the ocean and restore you to Rama.' Sita wondered how a little monkey could carry her across the ocean. To dispel her doubts, Hanuman began to magnify his form before her. She gazed at him with wonder and said, 'O Hanuman, I do not doubt your strength. But it is not right that you should carry me. On the way the demons may attack you with deadly weapons in the air. And you will have to fight them with a burden on your back. Besides, if you take me away, it will bring no credit to my husband. Let Rama come like a warrior, kill Ravana and then take me.'

'You are right,' said Hanuman. She gave him the Choodamani, the crest-jewel she had and said, 'In all my troubles this gem has been my consolation. I am sending this to him in the hope that he will come here very soon.' Hanuman respectfully received the token, went round the princess prostrated before her and took leave of her.

DESTRUCTION OF GARDEN

WHILE going out of the garden, Hanuman thought within himself. 'What can I do to instill courage into Sita and fear into Ravana? I should create a disturbance here and provoke the enemy to fight.' He began to uproot the trees, trample on the flower beds, and overthrow the roofs of the houses. The noise attracted the attention of the demon guards. Soon there was a big crowd armed with sticks and stones. The warriors came running to catch him. On seeing them, Hanuman jumped down and wrenching a huge rod from the gate, attacked them fiercely. Some of the guards went and reported the matter to Ravana. He was enraged. He ordered five mighty commanders to go with a big army and capture the monkey. But Hanuman pelted them with boulders, smote them with trees and killed them. Hearing of the death of his commanders Ravana called his son Indrajit and said, 'You are a, great warrior. Even the gods tremble at the mention of your name. Go now and fight and return triumphant.'

Indrajit bowed and marched to the garden in a chariot drawn by four mighty elephants, and showered arrows on Hanuman. But, Hanuman rose in the sky and moved swiftly. None of Indrajit's arrows hurt him. Indrajit concluded that his enemy had perhaps got a boon from the gods that he could not be killed in the ordinary way. So, he discharged Brahmastra the potent missile of Brahma. At its very touch Hanuman lay bound and helpless. The soldiers ran and bound him hand and foot with ropes so that he might not rise again. They did not know that the Brahmastra would lose its power once bonds of earthly material touched. it. Indrajit knew it, but it was too late to stop them. Hanuman also knew it. If he had wished, he could have broken himself loose from the ropes. But, he submitted himself to be led into the presence of Ravana so that he might have an idea of Ravana's palace and his mind.

BURNING OF LANKA

HANUMAN was taken to the court and brought in front of Ravana. Ravana commanded his ministers to question Hanuman and find out who he was. On being questioned, Hanuman addressed Ravana directly, 'I am a messenger from Sri Rama. I am one of those monkeys who have been commanded to find out where the princess Sita is kept hidden. I have found her.

'I will now go back and give this information Rama. What he will do next is not for me to say. But, I advise you to restore her to Rama and seek his forgiveness. You and your kingdom are in immediate danger of being destroyed on account of your crime.'

Ravana was wild with rage. He ordered that Hanuman should be put to death at once. But Vibhishana, his younger brother, intervened and pointed out

that it would be improper to kill a messenger. Then Ravana ordered
Hanuman's tail to be set on fire.

The demons led Hanuman out of the hall, wrapped old
rags round his tail, soaked it in oil and set fire to it. He was paraded

through the streets of Lanka. A big mob followed this procession, jeering, taunting Hanuman and dancing in joy. Sita was informed of the fate of Hanuman. Sita prayed to Agni, the god of fire, 'O Agni, may he feel no heat at all. Be cool to him.' So the fire never hurt Hanuman. He proceeded from street to street quietly noting the secrets of the fortified city. 'But what a miracle is this?' he thought: 'The fire is burning brightly but my tail feels very cool.' On finishing his survey he decided to teach a lesson to the demons. Suddenly, he shrank in size and shook off the ropes that bound him. He escaped and got on top of the roof of a house. Then he set fire to the roof and ran on the top of all houses in the street from one end to another. All of them caught fire and their inmates rushed out with their children; crying piteously. A strong wind began to blow and the flames spread through the entire city. Seeing the whole city burning, Hanuman was satisfied. He ran to the sea and drenched his flaming tail in the water. Suddenly, he had a painful doubt. Had the

fire destroyed Sita also? What a tragedy that would be! He ran to the garden and saw Sita sitting calmly under a tree. Bowing before her he said, 'Mother, I see you safe and sound. This is due to your power and my good fortune. Now give me leave to go.' He once more prostrated before her and took leave of her.

HANUMAN GIVES THE CHOODAMANI

HE then flew to one of the peaks in the mountain range and from there began his homeward flight. He flew straight as an arrow and reached the Mahendra mountain. The monkeys who were waiting for him jumped in joy saying, 'It is certain that he has succeeded.' As soon as he alighted, he first went to Jambavan and gave the news. All jumped with joy, saying 'Sita has been found.' They went in a group to Kishkindha and alighted near a protected park of the monkey king. They entered the park, drank honey and ate fruits disregarding the protests of the guards. The guards rushed to Sugriva and complained about the behaviour of the monkeys. Sugriva understood and said to the guards, 'Send them here at once.' Soon they were in the presence of Rama, Lakshmana and Sugriva. Hanuman bowed before them respectfully and said, 'I have seen the goddess of purity, Mother Sita. She is safe but is weeping for you.' He  placed the Choodamani which Sita had given, in the hands of Rama. Rama burst into tears when he saw it. He said to Hanuman, 'You have achieved what none else could. How can I repay you?' and embraced him warmly.

VIBHISHANA'S SURRENDER

IN Lanka, Ravana learnt through his spies that a vast army of monkeys was camping on the sea-shore. He summoned his ministers for advice. To please him they all praised him and declared he was unconquerable. But only one, Vibhishana his younger brother, said boldly that they had underestimated Rama. He advised his brother to give back Sita and make peace with Rama. Ravana, displeased with Vibhishana, said, 'We shall meet again tomorrow and consider the course of action.' The next morning the assembly met again.

'Don't you see, my brother.' said Vibhishana, 'since the time you brought Sita to Lanka, how bad omens are appearing. They are warnings to us.' Ravana said, 'You all know that I have brought Sita here from the forest. Such is my desire for her that sending her back is impossible. Moreover, the monkeys are camping on the other side of the ocean. It will be impossible for them to cross over. And even if they do, why should we fear them?' When Kumbhakarna, his another brother was consulted, he said, 'I think you have put yourself in great danger. You should have met Rama face to face and killed him before carrying off Sita. Now it is too late. What is the use of seeking our advice at this juncture? This is not the way a king should act'. Seeing his fond brother Ravana sad he said again, 'But have no fear, my brother, I will fight your enemies. I shall kill Rama and Lakshmana. Stop worrying and get ready for the war.' But, Vibhishana again appealed to Ravana: 'We have brought death in the form of Sita. So seek Rama's pardon and save our kingdom.' On hearing these words Ravana lost his patience and said, 'I have put up with your talk so far only because you are my brother. But, you are an utter disgrace to our race.' Vibhishana understood that it was not proper to remain with Ravana. He rose into the sky and made his way straight for Rama's camp with four of his trusted friends.

When the monkeys saw the five demons descending from the sky, they ran and informed Rama. Sugriva and others advised Rama not to trust these visitors. But, the intelligent Hanuman knew Vibhishana. He said that the very fact that Vibhishana had come there fearlessly, showed that he was sincere. He should be given an opportunity to explain his intention. Rama, who was listening to their different opinions, quietly spoke now, 'To him who seeks my protection saying, "I am yours," I offer refuge at once. That is a vow which I have taken and I cannot depart from it. Bring him here. Be it Vibhishana or Ravana himself, Shall I grant him protection.' Sugriva went and brought Vibhishana. His friendship was accepted by Rama and he was crowned the future king of Lanka.

CONSTRUCTION OF THE BRIDGE

THEN, Sugriva, Lakshmana and Vibhishana together discussed how they should cross the sea. For three days, Rama prayed to Varuna, the god of the ocean, for a passage. Since there was no response, Rama was enraged and he took up the Brahmastra in his hand and was about to hurl it on the ocean. Immediately, Varuna came out of the water and said with joined palms, 'O Rama, how can I give up my nature of being fierce, deep and unconquerable? It is not possible to part the waters and provide a dry passage. Instead I am willing to help you in another way. Let the monkeys build a bridge with the help of boulders and trees. I shall see that no creature of mine, whale or shark or crocodile, shall harm your army when it crosses the sea. I too shall help you to build the bridge.'

Thousands of monkeys set about the task with great enthusiasm. They went into the forest, uprooted trees and dragged them to the sea-side. They enjoyed rolling the boulders down the hill slopes to the water's edge. They jumped and danced, sang and laughed as they pulled out the rocks and trees. When enough materials were piled up, the great architect Nala started building the bridge. Under his direction long measuring tapes were held by bands of monkeys while he went forward with skilled workmen holding long poles to measure the depth at various places. It was a mighty undertaking. But, the entire monkey force worked hard and completed the bridge in just five days. The army crossed over to Lanka using the bridge.

ANGADA GOES AS A MESSENGER

RAMA sent for Angada and said to him, 'Prince, go to Ravana and give him a message from me.' Angada at once rose in the air and reached Ravana's palace. After introducing himself, he said, 'O King, I have come as Rama's messenger. Your end is fast approaching. If you choose to fight, be ready to lose everyone in Lanka.' Ravana flared up. 'Seize this monkey! Kill him!' he shouted. At once, two deomons caught hold of Angada. But, he rose up into the sky felling the demons with a mighty kick and with a single leap returned to his camp.

RAVANA'S BLACK MAGIC

RAVANA thought if somehow Sita could be made to yield to him, Rama would go back disgraced and broken-hearted. He thought of doing a black-magic. So he called a magician and asked him to produce a head to resemble that of Rama. He ordered the magician to wait near the Asoka garden with the head and a long sword. Then he went to Sita and announced to her boastfully that at last he had killed Rama: 'I have slain that insignificant human, I mean your husband. I need no longer beg you to become mine. You are mine now. Do you understand? Your husband is killed.' Saying so, he placed the head and the sword in front of Sita. Sita shrieked on seeing the head covered with blood and dust. She fell down unconscious. Meanwhile, a messenger came hurriedly to Ravana with a message from the ministers and generals that his presence was urgently required. He, therefore, left Sita to attend the assembly. When he left, the illusory head also vanished like smoke. Sarama, one of the demonesses around Sita, consoled her saying, 'No one has killed Rama. He is alive and safe. You have been deceived by magic. It was a magic head that they brought to you. Rama has reached Lanka and is preparing for the war.' Even as she was speaking, the noise of drums and trumpets sounded by the monkey army reached Sita's ears and filled her with joy.

BEGINNING OF THE WAR

RAMA ordered the monkey army to attack. They rushed forward and hurled huge boulders against the city walls and gates. The demons came out and attacked the monkeys. The monkeys uprooted trees and boulders to fight the demons. Thousands were killed on each side and the battle field was soaked in blood. The battle continued for a long time even after nightfall. Angada distinguished himself by attacking Indrajit and killing his charioteer and horses. Indrajit rose into the sky and making himself invisible, shot deadly serpent darts at Rama and Lakshmana. The arrows came hissing. The serpents bit the two princes all over their bodies and bound them. Rama and Lakshmana bled profusely and soon fell to the ground bound hand and foot. The monkeys scattered in fear seeing Rama and Lakshmana down. Indrajit thought Rama and Lakshmana were dead. He rushed to the presence of Ravana and declared that his enemies were no more alive. Ravana rejoiced to hear his son's triumph.

Meanwhile, the ocean and air were churned by a mighty wind and a celestial eagle burst into view. The monkeys looked at the sky and saw the eagle coming down flapping his wings. At the sight of eagle the serpents binding the brothers fled. The eagle passed his wings over the bodies of Rama and Lakshmana. Immediately, their wounds were healed and their strength returned. They rose refreshed as if from a long sleep. Wondering at this transformation, Rama asked the celestial visitor who he was. The eagle humbly said, 'I am Garuda, the king of birds and at my sight all serpents move away and at my touch all poison neutralized.' Seeing them fully recovered, the monkeys once again resumed their attack on Ravana's fortress. Ravana then sent many of his renowned generals. and were killed by the monkey heroes. At last Ravana himself mounted his chariot and came to the battlefield. Sugriva and others fought furiously against him. A fierce battle took place between Ravana and Hanuman. Ravana then challenged Rama and Lakshmana. Lakshmana fought heroically, but Ravana grasped a mightly missile called Sakti which Brahma had bestowed on him. He hurled it with all his might against Lakshmana. It came like a thunderbolt and struck Lakshmana on the chest. Lakshmana fell down unconscious. Hanuman carried him away to Rama and revived him. Then he pounced on Ravana and gave him such a blow with his fist that blood came out through his mouth, and nose. Rama now came into the field. Ravana could not stand the fierce onslaught of Rama. He was sorely wounded. His bow fell from his hands. His chariot was smashed. Deprived of everything, he stood helpless by before Rama. Rama took pity on him and said, 'You may go and rest now. You have fought creditably today. I give you leave. Take rest and come back tomorrow in another chariot with fresh weapons.'

RAMA KILLS KUMBHAKARNA

RAVANA was ashamed and as there was no other course left open for him, he beat a hasty retreat. His pride was humbled and he sat in his palace dejected. Suddenly a thought struck him. He ordered Kumbhakarna to be roused from his long sleep. The generals prodded Kumbhakarna with sharp instruments and goaded tuskers butted him But to no purpose. Then they placed beside him huge quantities of delicious food. Its fragrance woke him up. Brushing aside all the elephants and the demon who were standing by, he yawned loudly and sat up. Then he began to eat and orink. Heaps of meat of various kinds and large barrels of blood and wine were consumed by him. When his hunger was appeased, the demons explained the situation to him.

On hearing this, Kumbhakarna rolled his eyes in anger and cried, 'What! Is this true? I will first go and kill Rama and Lakshmana and then see my brother.' But, they persuaded him to see Ravana first and take instructions from him before going to meet the enemy.

Kumbhakarna agreed and marched into the presence of Ravana. Ravana, glad to see his brother, got down from his throne and embraced him. He informed him about all the events and begged him to save Lanka from the destructive hands of Rama. Kumbhakarna laughed and said, 'You need have no fear of any kind, while I am alive, my brother.' So saying, he marched to the battlefield with a number of chiefs. He roared his battle cry which sounded like thunder in the ears of the monkeys. Seeing the giant moving slowly toward them like a walking-mountain, the monkeys took to their heels in terror. Rallied by Angada, however, they came back again and tried to face Kumbhakarna. They attacked him with uprooted trees and threw several boulders but these missiles struck the giant's body and fell to pieces. Could no more The monkeys stand before Kumbhakarna. They fled in all directions to save their lives. But, Hanuman brought them back. They marched against Kumbhakarna and once more hurled their weapons on his body. A jagged rock from Hanuman's hand struck Kumbhakarna on his breast and he began to bleed. But, he unheedingly struck Hanuman with a lance who fell down spouting blood. Neela and others attacked again. Several monkey chiefs flew up and landed on the various parts of the giant's body and began to bite him with their teeth and tear

him with their nails. He tried to shake them off. But, they hung on to him. He plucked handfuls of them from above his body and put them into his mouth and swallowed them. Later, he rushed towards Rama ignorning the attacks of Lakshmana and others. A terrible duel followed between Rama and Kumbhakarna. Finding that ordinary arrows were useless against the demon, Rama discharged an arrow sacred to the wind-god. This weapon tore off Kumbhakarna's hands. Another arrow cut off his legs. He fell with a mighty crash. He was now an ugly creature devoid of arms and legs. And yet, he opened his cave-like mouth and with his long tongue swept many monkeys into it. Another arrow cut off his head from the trunk and swept it out of sight. The head rose to the sky and dashed itself against the gate posts of Lanka.

HANUMAN BRINGS SANJIVINI

WHEN Ravana heard of the death of his brother Kumbhakarna, he swooned. After he recovered, he lamented the loss for a long time. Seeing him so dejected, Indrajit, the son of Ravana, tried to console him saying, 'Why are you so sad and anxious while I am alive. You may take Rama and Lakshmana as already dead. You should not give way to despair as long as I am alive!' With these words, he mounted his chariot and drove to the battlefield. During the fight he flew into the air and became invisible. From nowhere came an incessant rain of arrows, on the monkeys below. They made a desperate attempt to fight back, but were powerless against an enemy they could not see. Finally, Indrajit discharged the sacred Brahmastra and the monkey army along with Rama and Lakshmana lay unconscious on the battlefield. Vibhishana, being a demon, was not affected by Indrajit's arrow. Jambavan, the great veteran of the monkeys, called Vibhishana and asked him to bring Hanuman near him. Vibhishana enquired, 'Why are you thinking of Hanuman instead of Rama and Lakshmana?'

'I am thinking of him', Jambavan replied, 'because if he is alive, it does not matter even if all others have fallen. But if he is dead, we are as good as dead and we may give up all hope.' Hanuman was deeply moved. Jambavan rejoiced to see Hanuman alive and said, 'Come here, my hero. You alone can save Rama and Lakshmana and the army. Go immediately to Sanjivini-Parvata, the hill of herbs between the Rishabha and Kailasa peaks in the Himalayas. There you will find four wonderful herbs which glow in darkness. These have marvellous healing powers.'

Hanuman rose in the sky and straight as an arrow made for the Himalayas. Finding some one looking for them, the herbs disappeared from sight. Hanuman was not the one who could be defeated in his purpose. He uprooted the entire peak, with all the herbs growing there, from the mountain and returned to Lanka. At the very smell of the herbs, Rama, Lakshmana and the other fallen monkeys leapt to life with their wounds healed.

DEATH OF INDRAJIT

THE battle resumed. The monkeys entered the city and set fire to it. Seeing this, Indrajit rushed out in his chariot. Through his magic he created an image of Sita and, catching it by the hair, appeared to kill Sita in the presence of the monkeys.

When the news was carried to Rama, he fell unconscious to the ground. Regaining consciousness a little later, he saw Vibhishana standing before him. 'Do not grieve,' said Vibhishana. 'Ravana will never allow Sita to be killed. What Indrajit destroyed was only an image. Having given up all hopes of defeating you by normal means, now Indrajit has gone to perform a sacrifice of great power. If he completes it, he will

be invincible. Therefore, let Lakshmana go immediately to obstruct the sacrifice.' Rama accordingly
sent Lakshmana accompanied by Vibhishana and
Hanuman. They reached the place where Indrajit was engaged in performing
sacrifice. Before he could complete it, Lakshmana attacked him fiercely. Mounting
his chariot Indrajit shot arrows at Lakshmana. Standing on Hanuman's shoulders
Lakshmana retaliated with sharper arrows. The two fought fiercely for a long time.
At last, Lakshmana used the Indrastra by which the head of Indrajit was cut off.
He fell dead.

THE FALL OF RAVANA

WITH the fall of Indrajit, Ravana was shattered. He wailed most piteously and
his sorrow turned into anger. His eyes became red with fury against Rama. He
started for the battlefield with the surviving chiefs. Forcing his way past Lakshmana,
Ravana came face to face with Rama. Both were great experts in wielding the bow, and
both had knowledge of celestial weapons. Therefore, the fight was long and equal.

One by one, Rama cut off Ravana's ten heads with his arrows. But, no sooner
was one head cut off than another grew to take its place. Matali, the charioteer of
Rama, who was sent by Indra with his chariot, whispered in Rama's ear, 'May I
remind you of the Brahmastra?' Rama took Brahmastra in hand, repeated the mantra
that gave it high power and hurled it with all might against Ravana.

The Brahmastra whizzed through the air emitting flame. It pierced the chest of Ravana. Ravana fell from his chariot. dead The demons could scarcely believe their eyes. The end was so sudden.

CORONATION OF RAMA

AFTER Ravana's death, Vibhishana was duly crowned king of Lanka. The message of Rama's victory was sent to Sita. After a bath and adorned with jewels, Sita was taken in a palanquin before Rama. Thousands of monkeys surged forward to get a glimpse of Sita. Sita got down from the palanquin and walked a little distance so that none was denied the privilege of seeing her.

At last, Sita reached her husband. Meeting him after a long time, she was overcome by joyous emotion. But, Rama seemed to be lost in thought. At length he, spoke, 'I have killed my enemy. I have done my duty as a true king. But, you have lived for a year in the enemy's abode. It is not proper that I should take you back now.'

Sita was shocked.' You have broken my heart' she said, 'only the uncultured speak like

this. Have you forgotten the noble family I come from? Is it my fault that the monster carried me off by force? All the time, my mind, my heart, and soul were fixed on you and you alone, my Lord!'

She turned to Lakshmana and said with tears streaming from her eyes, 'Prepare a fire for me. That is the only remedy for this sorrow of mine.' Lakshmana in suppressed anger, looked at Rama's face, but saw no sign of softening. He lighted a big fire. Sita reverently went round her husband and approached the blazing fire. Joining her palms in salutation, she said, 'If I am pure, O fire, protect me.' With these words she jumped into the flames, to the horror of the monkeys who stood on all sides watching the tragic sight. Then arose from out of the flames Agni, the fire-god, whom she had invoked. He lifted Sita from the flames unharmed, and presented her to Rama. 'Don't I know that she is spotless and pure at heart?' cried Rama, standing up to receive her. 'It is for the sake of the world that I made her go through this ordeal of fire, so that the truth may be known to all.'

Rama and Sita, now reunited, ascended the plane called Pushpaka along with monkey friends and

Vibhishana. Hanuman went in advance to inform Bharata of their arrival. As they flew in the sky, Rama pointed out to Sita, the spots where he and Lakshmana had wandered in the forest in search of her.

When Bharata saw Rama at a distance, a joyous cry went up. Bharata prostrated himself before Rama.

They all returned to Ayodhya. The city eagerly waited to receive them. Rama was crowned king and took up the reins of government much to the joy of his subjects. ✴